Detective Dan

by Vivian French

illustrated by Alison Bartlett

A & C Black • London

White Wolves Series Consultant: Sue Ellis,
Centre for Literacy in Primary Education

This book can be used in the White Wolves Guided Reading programme with
children who need a lot of support with reading at Year 3 level.

First published 2004 by
A & C Black Publishers Ltd
37 Soho Square, London, W1D 3QZ

www.acblack.com

ISBN 0-7136-6861-X

A CIP catalogue for this book is available from the British Library.

Printed and bound in Spain by G. Z. Printek, Bilbao.

Contents

For Ross

Chapter One

Dan and Billy were best friends. They walked to school together every morning. Every afternoon they ran home together. They did everything together.

One Monday afternoon Dan came out of school very slowly.

"What's the matter, Dan?" his mum asked.

"Someone threw his lunch box on the floor," Billy told her.

Mum said, "Maybe it just fell off the shelf."

"Mrs Harper said Dan was untidy," Billy said.

"Yes," said Dan. "And I'm *not* untidy!"

Dan stamped crossly all the way home.

On Tuesday afternoon Dan came out of school even more slowly.

"What's the matter, Dan?" his mum asked.

"Someone threw his lunch box on the floor *again*," said Billy.

"I'm sure they didn't mean to," said Mum. "Did you eat your sandwiches?"

"No," said Dan. "I didn't feel hungry."

"Mrs Harper says Dan is getting *very* untidy," Billy told Mum.

"Yes," Dan said. "And she said that I shouldn't talk to Minnie!"

"Is that the school cat?" Mum asked.

"Yes." Dan frowned. "It's not fair. I don't mean to talk to Minnie, but Minnie always comes to talk to me!"

Dan stamped crossly all the way home again.

On Wednesday afternoon Dan and Billy rushed out of school.

"Someone nibbled Dan's sandwiches!" Billy told Mum.

"Yes," said Dan. "Someone threw my lunch box on to the floor. Someone threw everything out of it. Someone nibbled one of my sardine sandwiches, and I'm *hungry*!"

"What did Mrs Harper say?" asked Mum.

"I didn't tell her," Dan said.

"Why not?" Mum asked.

"She was cross," Dan said. "Minnie came into the classroom with me."

"Mrs Harper said Dan let her in, but he didn't." Billy said. "Minnie just followed him."

"We'd better have a great big tea," said Mum.

"With extra big sardine sandwiches!" said Dan.

Chapter Two

On Thursday morning Dan walked slowly along the path.

"I think I should hide my lunch box today," he told Billy. "Then no one can eat my sardine sandwiches."

"You haven't got sardine sandwiches today, Dan," Mum said. "I had to make you cheese instead."

Billy suddenly stopped.

"I know!" he said. "I'll be a detective! I'll look for clues. I'll find out who pushed your lunch box off the shelf and tell Mrs Harper. Then she won't blame you."

"*Yes!*" said Dan, and they ran all the way to school.

Dan and Billy ran into the playground.

"Look!" said Billy. "There's Minnie!"

Dan called, "Minnie! Puss, puss, puss!"

Minnie came running. She ran in and out of Dan's legs, and round and round his school bag. But when he tried to pick her up she wriggled and struggled.

Mrs Harper walked past them.

"Now, Dan," she said. "I don't want Minnie in school. Put her down, please."

Dan put Minnie down, and she ran away at once.

"Why doesn't she like me today?" Dan asked.

"I'll find out!" Billy told him. "I'm a detective!"

"You've got to find out about my lunch box first," Dan said.

When it was time for lessons Dan and Billy hurried inside.

They put their lunch boxes on the shelf outside the classroom, and sat down at their table for quiet reading time.

"Look out for clues!" Billy whispered.

Dan nodded.

"No whispering!" Mrs Harper said.

Billy put his hand up.

"Please may I go to the toilet?" he asked.

Mrs Harper frowned. "Do you have to, Billy?"

"Yes, Mrs Harper," Billy said.

"What were you doing?" Dan whispered when Billy came back.

"Looking for clues," Billy whispered. "You go next!"

Dan put his hand up.

"Please may I go to the toilet?"
he asked.

Mrs Harper frowned again.

"Do you really have to go?"

Dan nodded.

"Did you see anything?"
Billy whispered
when Dan
came back.

"My lunch
box is still
there," Dan
whispered back.

Mrs Harper folded her arms. "Billy and Dan," she said. "I do *not* like whispering in my classroom! You two can stay inside at playtime!"

Billy smiled. "Thank you, Mrs Harper," he said.

Mrs Harper looked at him in surprise.

"What are you two up to?" she asked.

"Nothing, Mrs Harper," Billy said.

"Billy's a detective," Dan explained. "He's going to find out who's been throwing my lunch box on to the floor."

"I see," Mrs Harper said. "Well, no more whispering! And you can sit in here and read *quietly* at playtime."

Chapter Three

When it was playtime Dan got his book and sat down. Billy sat down until Mrs Harper had gone out, and then he jumped up again.

"Let's look for fingerprints," he said.

"How?" Dan asked.

Billy thought for a moment. "We'll put chalk dust on all the lunch boxes," he said. "Then we'll see everybody's fingerprints!"

"Won't it be messy?" Dan asked.

"We need to find a clue," Billy told him.

"OK," said Dan.

Billy picked up the board rubber, and dusted chalk dust over the lunch boxes.

"There!" Billy said. "Now we'll see *everybody's* fingerprints!"

At dinner time Billy and Dan watched carefully as everybody else collected their boxes.

"*Yuck!*" said Molly. "My lunch box is all dusty!"

"*Atchooo!*" sneezed Ben. "So is mine!"

All the children began blowing at the chalk dust.

"*Atchoo! Atchoo! Atchoo!*" they sneezed.

Mrs Harper came to see what was going on.

"Dan!" she said crossly.
"Is this something to do with you and Billy?"

Dan looked at Billy. Billy looked at the floor.

"We were looking for fingerprints," Dan explained.

Mrs Harper frowned her most terrible frown. "I think," she said, "you two had better stop being detectives *right now!*"

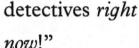

At the end of the afternoon
Dan and Billy walked out of
school very slowly indeed.

Mum was waiting at the gate.

"What's the matter now?" she
asked. "Did somebody eat your
sandwiches again?"

"No," Dan said. "Nobody took my lunch box today."

"Mrs Harper was very, very, *very* cross," Billy said.

Dan nodded.

"We had to stay in at dinner time," Billy said.

"Mrs Harper didn't read us a story in the afternoon," Dan said.

"Everyone had dusty jumpers," Billy said. "So they were cross too."

"It's not fair," said Dan, and he stamped all the way home.

Billy walked home behind him.

Chapter Four

On Friday morning Dan plodded along very slowly to school.

"Cheer up," Mum said. "I made you an extra-big sardine sandwich today."

Dan didn't cheer up.

"I'll be a detective again!" Billy said. "I'll find out about your lunch box!"

"No," Dan said. "I don't like that game. I don't like it at all!"

Dan didn't cheer up when Minnie came to meet him in the playground.

He didn't cheer up when he went inside.

He put his lunch box on the shelf, and sat down at his table with a sigh.

"Cheer up, Dan," said Mrs Harper.

Dan didn't answer. He picked up his book for quiet reading.

Billy looked at Dan, and then he picked up his book too.

Dan was very quiet all morning. When it was time for dinner he stayed sitting at his table. Billy stayed too.

"Come along, you two," said Mrs Harper. "Get your lunch boxes and zoom down to the dinner hall!"

"I'll get your lunch box, Dan," Billy said. He went out of the door, and stopped dead.

There was only one lunch box left on the shelf.

"Mrs Harper!" Billy shouted, "Dan's lunch box has gone *again*!"

Mrs Harper found Dan's
empty lunch box by the waste bin.

Dan found his carton of drink
behind a chair.

Billy found Dan's apple and
biscuit under a table.

There was no sign of Dan's extra-big sardine sandwich anywhere.

"Dear me," Mrs Harper said. "Dan, I think you'd better have a school dinner."

"You can share my sandwiches," Billy said.

"No thank you," said Dan.

Chapter Five

After dinner Mrs Harper asked
everyone to sit down. She asked
if anyone had taken Dan's
sandwich. All the children shook
their heads.

"What kind of sandwich was it,
Dan?" Mrs Harper asked.

"Sardine," said Dan.

Everyone made a face.

"No one likes sardines except
Dan," Billy said.

"Is that true?" asked Mrs Harper.

Everyone nodded.

Mrs Harper looked at Dan. "Well, Dan! I don't know what to say. Maybe we do need a detective after all!"

Dan didn't answer. He was looking through the open classroom door.

"Are you listening to me, Dan?" Mrs Harper asked.

Dan suddenly smiled a huge smile. "I know who ate my sandwich!" he said. "It was *Minnie!*"

Mrs Harper shook her head.

"Oh no, Dan. I'm sure she didn't!"

"Yes!" said Dan. "She liked me on Monday. On Tuesday she followed me into school. On Wednesday my sandwich was nibbled. But she didn't like me yesterday, and yesterday I had a cheese sandwich. Today I had sardines again, and she *did* like me." Dan looked sad.

"That's what I thought. It isn't me she likes, though. It's my sardine sandwiches! Look!" And he pointed.

Mrs Harper looked. So did Billy. So did all the children in the class.

Minnie was up on the lunch box shelf. She was walking in and out of the empty boxes, sniffing. Suddenly, she stopped.

"That's my box!" Dan whispered.

Minnie pushed at the box with her paw.

CRASH!

It fell on to the floor, and opened. Minnie jumped down and climbed inside. She was purring loudly.

"Well, I never," said Mrs Harper. "Well done, Detective Dan!"

The children cheered.

"Next week you'd better keep your lunch box *inside* the classroom!" Mrs Harper said.

Dan nodded.

Mrs Harper smiled at him.

"I'm sorry I said you were untidy. And I'm sure Minnie is too!"

At the end of Friday afternoon Dan came jumping out of school.

"You've cheered up!" Mum said.

"*Yes!*" said Dan. "Come on, Billy! Let's *run!*"

"OK," said Billy. He looked at Mum.

"Did you know?" he said. "Dan's the best detective *ever!*"

And he and Billy ran all the way home together.

About the author

Vivian French spent ten years working as an actor and writer in children's theatre, and toured all over England and Wales. She has been a storyteller in schools for many years and started writing stories down in 1990. Since then, Vivian has had over two hundred books published. She has four grown-up daughters and now lives in Edinburgh, though she isn't totally sure where she'd really like to live yet.

Other White Wolves titles you might enjoy ...

Buffalo Bert, the Cowboy Grandad by Michaela Morgan

Buffalo Bert isn't like other grandparents. He's always doing crazy things. Sunny thinks that Bert is great – until her new friends come along ...

Treasure at the Boot-fair by Chris Powling

Cal is helping out on Mr Jessop's stall. It's a tough job – he needs to be quick and clever and fair. Especially when something valuable turns up for sale.

 # White Wolves